MY LAUGH-OUT-LOUD LIFE

# THE BIG BREAKOUT

## Burhana Islam

KNIGHTS OF

*For my very own Samwise,*
*I couldn't have carried this without you.*

By Super-Spy and Secret Agent, Yusuf Ali Khan (age: almost 10 and a half)

My name, should you **DARE** to know it, is Yusuf Ali Khan (the first, the last, and the one and only). You may remember me from missions such as **OPERATION: RUIN MY SISTER'S WEDDING**, deadly negotiation tactics with the infamous Masked Trickster, and being on the 5B-Revenger's task force when securing my rightful place to take over the world (AKA our **WHOLE SCHOOL** or aka maybe just becoming form captain of our class).

That's right; I'm a little bit of a **HUGE DEAL** and (entirely by accident) I'm one of the most **POWERFUL** people in school right now. But that's enough about me: it's time to tell you about my most dangerous mission yet. Yep, you guessed it. Within these very pages, you'll find secret intelligence found nowhere else in the entire galaxy. This highly classified guide entails the story of a runaway Nanu, the ultimate school/prison-break attempt, and my colossal battle for Affa's human bean.

Confused?
I thought so.
So let me break it down for you:

I may have made a teeny-tiny, weeny-eenie, itsy-bitsy deal with the devil's best friend (my DB¹). My sister Affa is going to have a baby and it's coming in less than two weeks! Affa has decided to get the baby delivered to Newcastle instead of Manchester because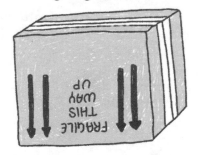

1. Affa's husband

she's on her own over there[2], and DB has left me in charge. Yes, me. What was he thinking, right? He's given me specific instructions too. I am no longer a mere man-of-the-house or just a form captain. This is my journey to evolving into **UNCLE MATERIAL**.

Only open if you think you can **HANDLE MY TRUTH**.

2. Her other side of the family have gone on a holiday to Bangladesh for two months.

# CHAPTER 1

At first, I thought I had dreamt it; it was just me and Affa in the sitting room, and she was snoring away on the sofa, being no help at all whatsoever. The curtains were half-closed, the door half-open, and a jar of almost-finished Nutella was eyeing me suspiciously. Affa had said that if I even thought about touching it, she'd break my legs. I'd been taking her threats VERY seriously recently, especially when it came to food. I only had the guts to lick a little bit. There was no telling what she was capable of when SHE activated HULK-MODE.

Anyway, there was no way on planet Earth, the Sun, the stars, and the galaxies beyond that there was another lifeform present in this room with us.

No way.

I had just imagined it. That had to be it, right? What else could've possibly been slithering away inside Affa's tummy, making its way towards the baby's fleshy den? It was nothing, right? My eyes had deceived me. They were only playing tricks. My glasses just needed a squeaky clean. Yeah, that's right.

Just as I almost believed it, IT HAPPENED AGAIN!
**HOLY SNOTBALLS!**
There it was: THE WIGGLE!

I jumped to catch my breath, trying not to swallow the waterfall of sweat dripping from my nose. Whatever this abomination was, it was wading itself deeper into Affa's bump. With no choice but to roll my stinky P.E. socks higher up my arms for protection, I got to work the way only an experienced Iron-Bhai scientist could. With a knife and fork at the ready (trying desperately not to vomit), I plunged my mechanical tools deeper into the Epaderm pot[1], waiting for the perfect moment to strike.

1. I have eczema. If you know, you know.

Come on. Come on! COME ON!

But the wiggle had disappeared again, just as quickly as it had come. It obviously knew I was a threat – even if it couldn't see me through Affa's dress. I needed to be faster, I needed to pee, and I needed to trap it quickly, but how could I trap something that looked like it was concealed under human skin? OH WHY, OH WHY DIDN'T THEY TEACH US THESE THINGS IN SCHOOL?!

I lowered the knife and fork towards where I suspected the presence had burrowed itself. Suddenly, my heart jumped full throttle to my throat, as the creature itself tried to communicate with me in its strange, unearthly language.

**KHAAAAAA - SHOOOOOO. KHAAAAAAA - SHOOOOOOO. KHAAAAAA - SHOOOOOOO.**

Oh, wait. False alarm. That was just Affa's snoring.

Focus, Yusuf. Focus. It'll come back any minute now. I'd examined its patterns of movement for a whole 6.33 minutes, so I was an expert at knowing when it would emerge from its current habitat.

By the way, if you were wondering why I was taking this job of protecting Affa and her bean (the new soon-to-be baby of the family) so seriously, it's because DB told me he's doing some very important training and won't be back until next weekend. Let's be real: it's no secret that if

3

I had to choose between Affa's life and a half-eaten Jaffa Cake, we'd be preparing for Affa's janazah[2] right now.

**ARGGGHHHHHH!**

The WIGGLE was back with a vengeance!

It was too bad that the man-of-the-house didn't run AWAY from fear. No way. He ran towards it!

"For the human bean!" I whispered, my nose almost touching the place Affa's belly button would likely be.

But at that moment, the WORST POSSIBLE THING happened. It was more frightening than THE WIGGLE, more fearsome than Nanu, and more threatening than Amma with a slipper!

The BEAST itself had awoken and let out a **TERRIFYING ROAR!**

2. Funeral

4

# CHAPTER TWO

"YUSUF!" Affa screamed, smashing a pillow against my face to send me sprawling across the floor. "WHAT THE ACTUAL FUDGECAKES ARE YOU DOING?"

Affa's hair was electric, the scarf around her neck all twisted, and her eyes jumped wildly from me to erm . . . ME! There was no doubt about it: this She-Hulk was on the warpath and it didn't matter that she had a baby in tow! I needed to initiate damage control FAST.

Fixing my glasses and crawling on all fours, I took refuge behind the sofa closest to the window.

"Affa!" I yelled, laser-scanning my surroundings quickly for a defence mechanism. Taking all the cushions I had left, I created a fort of protection to soften any incoming blows. "You need to calm the SNOTBALLS down. You hear me?"

5

"Calm down?!" Affa bellowed, hurtling a blanket in my direction. "I'M COMPLETELY CALM!" [3]

"Errr," I tried to peek over the sofa, but a flying Pikachu (not mine . . . okay, maybe mine) shot past me, narrowly missing my ear. When I was brave enough to try a second time, Affa locked eyes on me like a python on its prey.

Bad idea. BAD IDEA!

I ducked back into the safety of my fortress, peering out for emergencies only.

"Why were you trying to eat my baby?!" Affa hissed with a dangerous glint in her eye. "When did you become a cannibal?!"

"Are you kidding me?" I squealed. "How can you accuse ME of EATING YOUR BABY when it's literally in your tummy?"

Affa really was unreasonable these days. What had gotten into her?

There was a rustle and a rummage from behind me.

"Who hovers over their sister with a greasy knife and fork?" She paused, probably looking for more ammunition. "What else am I supposed to think?"

"I was trying to PROTECT you and the baby!" Maybe if I said it louder, she'd believe me more. Good plan.

3. FYI, Affa was the **TOTAL OPPOSITE** of **CALM** – mega gulp!

Let's try that. "THERE WAS SOME SUSPICIOUS ACTIVITY IN YOUR BELLY!"

Well, that didn't work because . . . INCOMING!

Another one of Affa's victims dropped dead to the floor. This time, it was an onion ring.

"How are you going to protect something you were going to eat, huh?"

Clearly, Affa had underestimated my relationship with chicken wings.

She wasn't stopping either. "The thing that was moving WAS the baby, you fool!"

OH! That made sense! Why didn't I think of that before?

Anyway, this had to end NOW. Stuffing one cushion up my jumper and using another as a Captain America shield, I made the decision to come face-to-face with the enemy. I could do this. No! I WOULD do this! I just had to explain to Affa politely that there was a LITTLE MISUNDERSTANDING when it came to the science of babies.

That was all, right?

Since the shelling had finally stopped, now was my time to strike (up a conversation, obviously). I wasn't foolish enough for anything else.

Tossing the fallen onion ring into my mouth, I turned to her with all the confidence I had left (which was about exactly zero, by the way).

"Affa, please," I said weakly. "Forgive me for not knowing where babies come from." I donned my best puppy dog eyes. "Until you came along, I'd never seen a baby on the inside before. Can you find it in your heart to forgive me?"

But at that moment, Affa swivelled her head and gasped, pointing to the evidence of my past-crimes.

## RED ALERT! RED ALERT!

I needed to get the BIG GUNS out! NOW NOW NOW!

AFFA HAD NOTICED!

She turned her head slowly towards me and whispered demonically. "Did you eat my Nutella?"

With nothing left to save me, I tried calling the only person I knew who could help.

"NAN-"

# CHAPTER THREE

"Wake up, Eesoof. Come on now, beta." Nanu's voice sounded light and airy, almost like an angel from the gates of Jannah[4] itself.

I felt Amma's hands on my cheek, all warm and fuzzy.

Where was I? What was happening to me?

"What possessed you to hit him that hard, Tammy?" Amma was asking, but she felt so far away. "I know you're having a child, beti, but why did you have to hit mine like that?"

4. Heaven

I should've probably opened my eyes, but I just loved this feeling so much that I was practically forced to drag the moment out. My body was holding me hostage and there was nothing I could do about it. Oh well, I guess this was just what love felt like. No wonder I was trying to hold onto it a bit longer. God only knew when it would happen next.

"I don't know what got into me," Affa said. Another rustle and a rummage came from her direction. More ammunition perhaps? She wouldn't dare in front of the grown-ups. Would she? "I honestly didn't think he'd slip on a cushion and hit his head on the wall like that." She paused. "He'll be fine. Don't worry."

**CRUNCH, CRUNCH, CRUNCH!**

Trust Affa to eat her way through my deathbed moment. Had she no shame? What would people say and, more importantly, what was she eating?

And on that **CRUNCH,** it was showtime. I still had to get myself out of trouble, remember? It wouldn't be too long before Affa accused me of being a baby-muncher. I had no choice but to get there first.

Opening my eyes slowly, I reached half-blindly for Affa's hands. I needed to be convincing. The best super-spies always were after all.

"Ammu-jan," I said weakly. I WAS JUST TOO

GOOD AT THIS! Somebody stop me! "Why doesn't Affa love me anymore?" I tried to force a lone tear out of my eyelids, but I think I might have just looked constipated.

"Told you he'd be okay," Affa said, untangling her fingers from mine and reaching for another onion ring. "Anyway, your little antics are beginning to make sense."

I shot up, almost colliding into the dangling tasbeeh[5] around Nanu's neck.

"What do you mean 'my antics'?"

Amma raised an eyebrow.

"I mean," I said, coughing slightly and trying to fumble back down very UN-dramatically. "Whatever do you mean, oh favourite and beloved sister of mine?"

"She means your attention-seeking," Nanu began, eyeing me suspiciously. "Eesoof Ali Khan, are you perhaps a little envious that you're not going to be the baby of the family anymore?"

## HOLD UP ONE NANO-SECOND, NANU!

"Do you mean to tell me YOU of all people Nanu (the person I trust most in this whole entire galaxy) . . ." My words were stumbling with flabbergasted-ness. "You think I, Yusuf Ali Khan (the first, the last and the one and only), Form Captain and Man-of-the-House, not

5. Prayer beads

11

to mention me beating Bashir in the Qu'ran competition last weekend, you believe that I WANT to be a baby?"

Who were these people? Had they no idea what I had been through to earn my badges?

Amma stared at me blankly, not even bothering to come to my defence, so Affa landed the blow instead.

"It's just . . ." she looked at me like I was carrying some nasty flesh-eating disease, torn between following HUGS LAW and running a whole kilometre just to get away from me. "I get it, Yusuf. Things are going to be changing around here and it's a lot for you to handle, but acting like a baby to get our attention isn't the way to do it."

## ARE YOU KIDDING ME?!

I could feel my ears prickling and my face burning up.

"Yusuf, baba," Amma began, but I couldn't let her continue. I had to put a stop to this foolishness.

Me? A baby? No way was I letting all my cool points go in 113 seconds flat. No way at all.

"I'm a little old to be called 'baba' now. Don't you think

so?" I straightened myself up and made myself Captain America confident. "If anyone's being babyish, it's Affa – since she actually has one in there."

Affa waddled back to the sofa, swiping the Nutella jar on her way back. "Look, Yusuf. We're not having a go at you."

"We're not?" Nanu asked, settling herself down beside Affa.

Amma laughed. She obviously wasn't taking this very seriously at all! Didn't she know my reputation was on the line?

"We're just saying that you're about to become an uncle soon," she sighed. "This kid, well, he's going to look up to you."

Amma and Nanu nodded with her. Traitors. So much for standing by the man-of-the-house.

"You need to up your game, bro. Being uncle-material isn't easy. Plus, your DB is depending on you. I don't think he'll be happy to hear that you fried chicken-ed your nephew with a knife and fork, will he?"

I shook my head. With Affa's delivery date still over a week away, at least I had more time to step up.

"Yusuf?" Affa asked, as Amma and Nanu left the room. "You don't know where babies come from, do you?"

Of course I didn't, but being uncle-material meant

that I didn't want her to know that.

I did a quick Sheikh Google rewind in my head from when I first investigated the matter.

"Affa, Affa, Affa," I tutted. "If you keep asking silly questions, I'm literally going to send you back to the womb."

There! That should do it.

Yusuf:1 Affa:0

# CHAPTER FOUR

"What do you mean things are changing?" Aadam clapped his hands to his cheeks and pulled his school jumper over his mouth. "Why can't things ever just stay the same?"

"It's not Yusuf's fault," Mustafa chimed in, putting his packed lunch back in his bag. "Mum says that he hasn't realised yet that most things can be solved with a 'simple conversation'. Aaaaand he's just got a weird family."

To be honest, Mustafa wasn't exactly lying there. Our bloodline put the WE in weird.

"Hey!" Aadam chirped, patting me on the back with a thump. "I am his family!"

The three of us walked towards our spot in the corner of the yard. The school bell for the start of the day would ring soon, so we had to make the most of the precious little time we had together.

"I said what I said," Mustafa nodded. "Anyway, what's the plan?"

"Well," I began, scratching my head, but Aadam had other ideas.

"Well nothing!" he interrupted, waving his hands.

"We've done so much already! Your minions need to be more grateful."

Did Aadam just call Affa, Nanu and Amma my 'minions'? If he valued his life, he would know never to utter those words out loud in their presence.

"What do you mean?" I asked, deciding against warning him. Who knows? It might be fun to watch.

"What do you mean 'what I do mean'?" Aadam pulled out my old Spider-Bhai campaign poster.

"Whoaaaaa," I said, beaming at my handsome face[6], which was stuck onto the special edition Iron Spider

Suit. "You kept it. Give it to me now, please!" I tried snapping the paper off him, but he was too fast and too serious.

"Look at the things we've done for the greater good already! We can't add anymore to the plan when we haven't even finished some of the stuff on the list yet!"

6. Amma said that I wasn't called Yusuf for no reason.

# Aadam, Mustafa and Yusuf's Plan for World Domination (Mostly Aadam)

- 'Fish and Chip Friday' to now become 'Masala Fish and Chip' Friday (to cater for the caramel community)
- Fun days before religious festivals like Eid and the World Cup instead of just Christmas
- Scrap eggs at Easter and add samosas instead (they're more nutritional, obviously)
- At Christmas time, instead of Secret Santa, have Secret Sahaba and raise the stakes to £1.50 for everyone who wants to take part so we can get some good treats
- At Halloween, instead of dressing up like devils, stone them instead (still working on it)
- At Wet-Break, mobilise the school-cinema task force for Year 4 - Year 6 so they can watch an episode of Spongebob Squarepants or Pokemon (teachers can quietly sip their cups of tea in the staffroom in peace - what's not to like?)
- ~~Same as above for Year 1, 2 and 3 - they can watch Shrek, Cars, Encanto and Toy Story. If anybody stepped a toe out of line, they'd be punished~~ SEVERELY ~~by being forced to watch Frozen against their own will (give Aadam's Disney+ password to the teachers)~~[7]

7. Okay, so this one was a no-go. One of the Year 1's had nightmares for seven days straight when Mr Blobby popped up in an advert break.

"What more can we realistically change before I go to secondary school?" Aadam stuffed the poster back in his bag, wayyyyy out of my reach. "Year 7 is a big deal, you know. I heard they flush your head down the toilet over there if you're not cool enough. I heard there's a ghost haunting the back building too. I've just got so much to think about already."

For a second, Aadam flushed as pink as an undercooked chicken before he went back to his usual skin colour.

"We could have more reading time?" Mustafa asked. "That's doable."

"Guys, we need to focus! I need a game plan." I leaned against the wall and tried hard to think. It wasn't a skill I had exactly mastered yet. "Look, I got less than two weeks to become uncle-material, but I don't know even what that means. I tried Googling it, but Google was more confused than I was."

"Well my Dad's an uncle to you," Aadam said. "We need to make a list of things he does for you."

"The problem is that I can't think of any." I had actually thought about that yesterday when I was doing my investigations.

"Job done, then," Mustafa said with a thumbs up. "Phew. Glad we sorted that out before any of us got into serious trouble, OR WORSE, had to face my Mum."

Aadam didn't look like he was convinced. "What about that time when . . . nope, that was me." His eyes went funny as he popped into a thought bubble of his own. I guess uncle-material had that effect on people. "What about . . . nope, me again. I think I might need to have a word with Dad."

"While you do that," Mustafa began, pointing towards the gates, "We'd better prepare for trouble."

He was right.

We needed to activate defence mode and fast because Sairah and Saleem were making their way towards us. Worse still, they were waving copies of The 5B Times.

Oh maaaaaaaaan.

Here we go again.

# CHAPTER FIVE

Even though Sairah had said that she'd changed, I always got the feeling deep inside my bones that one day she'd backstab us all and return to her conniving ways. Well, thank God that today was NOT that day.

"A little samosa told me that you're in DESPERATE need of my help," Sairah said, tugging the plaits in her hair.

That's actually a nice greeting by her standards. Trust me.

Saleem nodded quickly after her. Sometimes he was so quiet that it was almost impossible to believe that the two of them were twins.

"If you're talking to samosas, I think you're the one in desperate need of help, not me," I said.

Yes, I actually said that out loud.

Yes, I regretted it instantly.

Yes, my heart did a real-life somersault.

Aadam was a little braver. "Are we just going to talk about samosas all day or are you going to tell us your plan?"

Sairah raised her eyebrow and Mustafa melted away behind me.

PSPSPS...

PSPSPS...

"I mean . . . you know . . . please?" Aadam backtracked, taking a step back to match.

"Ammu told us that our khala said that the lady at number 5 mentioned that the auntie on your street told her that you're going to have a baby." Saleem counted his fingers just to make sure he got that right. "Do you know if you're going to be an auntie or an uncle yet? Or is that a surprise?"

Sairah shook her head and rolled her eyes. "ANYWAYYYYY, I conducted a poll with a grand total of some very important people (me and Saleem here). We've made a list of all the things you have to do to become 'uncle-material.'"

"How did you know we were talking about that?" Mustafa asked, checking over his shoulders for spies.

Aadam tripped up, as he tried to kick his own shadow. Did he seriously believe that it would betray him? Since Year 6 were told they had SATs and had to 'prepare for big school', Aadam's not exactly been himself.

"Do you really need to ask?" she smiled. "Look Yusuf, I get it. You're Form Captain, man-of-the-house and you managed to beat Bashir at mosque last week, but that's just the tip of the samosa."

At that second, Aadam imploded – he just IMPLODED! "Unless we are EATING chicken samosas, I don't want to hear another soundbite about them." He looked down and patted his stomach. "They're just teasing you, bro." His tummy was so annoyed that it even growled back.

"What I mean to say is," Sairah continued, pressing forward. "Any 10-year-old can do these things. Let's be real."

WAIT ONE SMELLY MINUTE!

Did Sairah Rahma Miah truly, in her heart of hearts, deep down, believe that just ANYBODY could accomplish the honours I'd worked SOOOO HARD for?

No way. Not if I had anything to do with it.

She left me with no choice but to defend my name, my honour and my reputation. Nobody, and I mean NOBODY (except Affa and me) was allowed to ruin that.

"I got my pen licence in Year 3," I whispered

SO LOUDLY that only my glasses could hear me.

There! That should put her in her place.

Sairah was so shocked at my words that she pretended not to hear me. Yeah, I would do that too **LEST SHE FELT MY WRATH!**

"So, what you have to do now is make sure that you've done all the uncle things in all the most important parts of your life: home, school and mosque. Here." She passed me her notebook and some monopoly money. "You can pay me back in Oreos[8]. Don't worry."

At **HOME**, uncles must:
- Make sure everything is organised everywhere
- That people are looked after
- ~~That they are funny~~[9]

At **SCHOOL**, uncles must:
- Be responsible
- Make sure the teacher is okay at **ALL TIMES**
- Teach the class

At **MOSQUE**, uncles must:
- Clean the wudhu area

8. Oreos for monopoly money? That kind of exchange rate just didn't sit well with me.
9. Sairah had crossed this out, and written "never going to happen" ...obviously she was **WRONG**

23

- Give children money
- Write a speech about being good
- Have a beard

Aadam's jaw practically dropped to the floor and my legs started feeling funny.

"He's got to do ALL of that?" Mustafa said. "And go to Friday prayers? That's a LOT."

Sairah snatched back the notebook again. "There's nothing about Fridays here at all."

But Mustafa had already taken a crayon out of his pocket and scribbled over the sheet. "There is now."

"There's NO WAY I'll be able to do all that," I cried, trying to catch my tears before anyone noticed.

Sairah must have known she'd enlisted me for an impossible mission because she took the notebook back and said, "Maybe we should just stick to one from each instead."

"Guys," Mustafa whispered, making all our stomachs drop to the floor. He only ever spoke like that when we were in the danger zone.

I GASPED in HORROR as I read the headline for

The 5B Times, which had fluttered to the floor at that exact moment.

"BASHIR THE BASHER BITES BACK," I read, pleading to Sairah. There was no way the class bully was after me again. "SAY IT'S NOT SO, SAIRAH! SAY IT'S NOT SO."

Sairah tried to kick my hands off her shoes, narrowly missing my nose. Hold up – why was I on the floor? When did I get here?

Saleem peeled me off her. "You know she only publishes the truth now so–"

"Guys," Aadam whispered, almost in the EXACT way Mustafa had. "He wasn't on about the headline." Aadam pointed to the car park where the teachers usually emerged from their cars, like zombies at the first light of dawn.

"We got some visitors," Mustafa said slowly as four men in black and a woman with shades on walked towards us. "Something tells me that they're out for blood."

# CHAPTER SIX

"Yusuf Ali Khan," Miss Minchell squealed, sitting and standing on repeat in her wheelie chair. Somebody was feeling very indecisive right now. It didn't help that her hair was all wild, her eyebags were on the floor,  and her upper lip was twitching suspiciously. "Just make sure all your Maths, English, Science and Humanities books are in the cupboard under the sink and put some paper towels on top of them! Mustafa bring yours to the front and put them in plain sight, you hear me? Spread them out in different parts of the classroom so they're visible from ALL ANGLES!"

"Miss, yes, Miss!" Mustafa said, saluting her before fulfilling his orders.

"Miss, what about my Project-Based Learning book?" I asked, waving it like a flag. It had some of my best work in there. Surely the MI5 agents would want to see that.

"Oh my God," Miss shrieked. Finally, at least she'd come to her senses. "Put that right at the bottom and cover it with that soggy tea towel."

Never mind.

"Your wish is my command," I whispered. If I'd said it any louder, she would have probably exploded.

"Sairah! Have you finished marking the Maths books yet? We still have to do the Science ones!" Miss was whizzing across the classroom, snatching the glue sticks off Liam and Bashir who had dared each other to lick them.

"Nearly!" Her pen was scribbling furiously. "I'm almost done!"

"Keep her right, Saleem." Miss ordered. "It's 'THINK PINK' and 'GREEN TICKS'. Get that red pen[10] away from her. Heaven forbid!"

Saleem nodded shakily, blowing the red pen away from Sairah as if it was a venomous festering dead rat.

10. Miss has never used a red pen since the day one popped and leaked all over Saleem's arm. He passed out because he thought he had been stabbed and hadn't realised.

28

Suddenly, Miss' neck snapped towards me. Clearly, I was treading on dangerous waters right now. Yes, the classroom floor was definitely beneath my feet, but the way Miss was eyeing me up, I felt like it was only a matter of time before a giant octopus swallowed me whole.

"I can't believe I'm saying this," she began, shushing the entire class now. "Here's the thing: because you're Form Captain, you've been chosen to show our very special visitors around the school." Miss looked towards the ceiling and said quickly. "They'll be here any minute. God help us."

You know, as a humble champion of Islam and a hafidh-in-training, it's always great to see people turning to God in their time of need, especially when I'd been trying for all of zero seconds to convince her.

"So here are the rules," she said, her eyes darting back and forth from the corridor window. Her words were running at a hundred miles per minute. "Yusuf, memorise this:

- No speaking unless being spoken to
- Just smile and nod, but don't do that thing where you smile with all of your teeth
- Answer any questions in the most polite and best way possible, but keep the talking to a minimum

- Take them to the best parts of the school, but avoid the Year 1 corridor
- If at any time you feel like you'll question the school's integrity, just say you're not sure

"Get it? Got it? Good!"

Miss sped towards the door, keeping it closed firmly by the handle. "They're coming for you," she squeaked as a man and a woman in black suits, clipboards (NOT A CLIPBOARD!), and red pens walked slowly towards our door. "Oh dear God," she squeaked, planting a fake smile slap bang in the middle of her face.

"But Miss," I said weakly, glancing towards Mustafa for the Batman signal. Now was his time to save my day.

But Mustafa had his nose buried in a book. Traitor.

"Miss?" I whispered, just loud enough for her to hear. "Everything will be okay if I just try my best, right?"

**RIGHT?!**

Miss Minchell's shoulders rolled towards the floor as she turned towards me. If she wasn't careful, she'd pass out. "On this occasion, please just try a little bit better than your best." She looked me directly in the eye as if she had the power of hypnosis and I couldn't break away from her trance. "You can do that for me, right?"

Before I even got a chance to answer, the door clicked

open and all eyes were on me.

I turned one last time to
Mustafa who just about
mouthed "Inna lillahi
wa inna ilayhi rajeoon."
To Him we belong and, from
the looks of things, I'd be returning
to God sooner rather than later.

My abductors were here and
I had no choice but to take this path laid out before me.
If things ended badly (Liam and Bashir were drawing
their fingers across their necks as a threat), at least
I knew I'd go down like a hero who walked bravely into
the face of fire.

# CHAPTER SEVEN

"This, my special friends," I announced grandly to Inspector #1 and Inspector #2.[11] "This is the Biome."

At that very moment, I was no longer Yusuf Ali Khan, the Form Captain of 5B. As hard as it was to believe, within mere minutes of leaving the classroom, I had transformed into a milk chocolate version of Willy Wonka, and this dome of greenery was my wonderland.

"Behold the school's greatest secret hideaway project." I waved my hands in the air for dramatic effect, but nobody seemed impressed.

Tough crowd.

"Useless, I don't think . . ." The lady inspector began.

"It's Yusuf." I corrected her. I really hated the stupid autocorrect on the stupid sticker the headteacher made me wear. She could've at least double-checked the spelling of my name before printing it. Yusuf and

11. Before I left the classroom, Miss pretty much made it forbidden to call our special visitors MI5. She said they were inspectors and that they were inspecting EVERYTHING – even me.

'Useless' have less than NOTHING in common!

"Ahh sorry," she said with not an ounce of sorry inside her. "Is this place usually so . . . accessible?" She flicked her brown hair behind her ear.

I deceptively peeled the sticker off my jumper and nodded. "It's usually locked, but there are three secret passageways." I tried to peer at her clipboard, but she practically stuffed it up her nose for safe keeping. Gross. "You can use the air vent up there." I pointed towards the loose board on the ceiling. "But nobody's used that since a Year 1 kid got stuck in there and the caretaker had to poke her out with a pole before she hyperventilated."

"Excuse me?" The man-inspector suddenly stopped inspecting the plant in front of him.

"Don't worry. It didn't happen again that year - and it's only happened three times since then." I scratched my head thinking of the other routes. "Miss Minchell sometimes leaves it open when she's in a rush, so that's another way in. There was one time when Chompy, the school chameleon (he's over there)," I pointed to his little evergreen glass habitat, "Well he escaped and somebody hit the fire alarm because it was the only way we could search for him secretly without terrifying him with hordes of little humans. Miss Minchell made us pinkie swear not to tell anyone, but it was plastered all over The 5B Times before break even started. It didn't help that it was a fireman who found Chompy sunbathing on the school roof." I smiled at the thought. "Such good memories."

Inspector #2's jaw was wide open. "There's one more entrance. You said three, right?"

I nodded. "Yes, there is. You don't want to know the other one though. It involves the girls' toilets, the Masked Trickster and a whole wad of toilet roll."

The lady-inspector went pale, almost like she was going to vomit. "The 'masked' what?"

"HOLY SNOTBALLS!" I raised my hand to stop her in her speaking tracks and almost stumbled over myself. "History is repeating itself! I repeat HISTORY IS REPEATING ITSELF!"

The inspectors jumped at the sound of my alarm and huddled near the door like they were being held hostage.

I rushed over to the tank where Chompy should have been lazing peacefully, only to find that the lid was open, and his lair was empty. There was no doubt about it; a hungry chameleon was on the loose.

# CHAPTER EIGHT

"Don't move," I whispered to Inspector #2. "Not another millimetre." I crept my way towards them.

Both inspectors were breathing heavily, taking my word as law (as they should - being Form Captain had its benefits).

"W-wh-where is it?" the man-inspector said, his bottom lip quivering. He clung onto his blazer like a lifejacket. Now was definitely a bad time to tell him that Chompy was crawling stealthily up his shoulder.

I tried my best not to glare into his deep, beady eyes (Chompy, not the inspector). If I gave him the 'I'm-not-angry I'm-just-disappointed' look, he would probably bolt, and we'd have no choice but to raise the alarm[12].

The lady-inspector was a bit braver, snapping into investigation mode immediately. "Is there any particular reason why he's called Chompy?" She scoured the floor and the plants above her, not realising that the Chomp-master himself was behind her.

12. And FYI I don't mean the fire alarm.
I'm not making that mistake again.

I took a deep breath and began. "There was one time that—"

But it looked like she had changed her mind. "You know what? Don't tell me." She shuddered at the thought. It looked like some truths were meant to stay buried.

The only SLIGHT problem was that the grown-ups were like lanky trees compared to me. Somehow, I had to get them onto the floor without giving anything away. Luckily, quick-thinking was an under-used superpower of mine.

"I think now is the time to fall to our knees and pray," I said sensibly, taking their sleeves and guiding them to the floor.

Please let this work. Please, ya Rabb. Let this work!

They must've been so weirded out that they just followed my instructions without question. It simply wasn't possible to tell you what it was like to wield that kind of power. Here these super-spies were, taking orders from Yusuf Ali Khan. If that wasn't uncle-material, God only knew what was.

But the WORST possible thing happened at that VERY MOMENT!

The lady-inspector SHRIEKED from the top of her lungs when she caught sight of Chompy's tongue stretching for her earring.

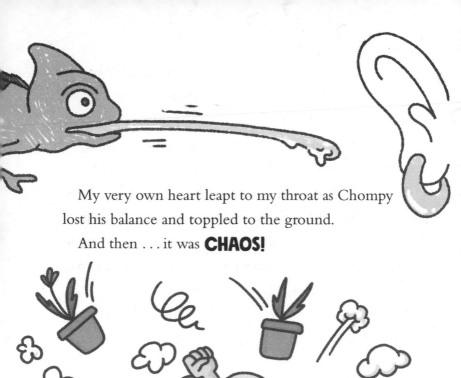

My very own heart leapt to my throat as Chompy
lost his balance and toppled to the ground.

And then . . . it was **CHAOS!**

Chompy bolted left, the man darted right, and the lady tripped backwards into the mini-forest of plants.

"EVERYONE NEEDS TO CALM DOWN! RIGHT NOW!" I screamed, tailing after the chameleon with all the life I had left in me. With no inhaler to hand and my oxygen levels beginning to borderline flatline, I dove into the spider-plants and just about caught Chompy by his tail.

Cradling the chameleon in my arms, I emerged from the jungle of tangled leaves. There was mud all over the place, compost scattered all over the floor, and the plants that didn't make it lay sprawled on the floor.

Worse still, Mrs Hedley (the school's formidable Miss Trunchbull-in-the-making) was at the door, glaring at me angrily.

**GULP!**

# CHAPTER NINE

It was official: **[OPERATION UNCLE STATUS]** had only been engaged for all of 23.66 minutes and already it was a disaster.

I sat on the chair outside ~~Miss Trunchbull's~~ Mrs Hedley's office, wobbling in shock.

"I'm okay," I whispered to myself, tapping my fingers. "It's just an office, just four walls and everyone will understand that I did what I had to do." My heart was racing, and a tiny bead of sweat was circling my nostrils like a live vulture in search of dead meat. I steadied my breathing. "I am not in trouble. I repeat: I am not in trouble."

"Bro," came a voice from behind me, giving me a FULL-ON out-of-body experience. Thankfully, I just about caught my soul on its way out. "You're in BIG TROUBLE." Mustafa finished, appearing out of the plants behind me.

"Yeah," Aadam agreed, appearing beside him.

In all the madness, I'd completely forgotten it was break-time. That was obviously the only way Mustafa and Aadam could've escaped the clutches of the classroom to warn me of a greater evil.

"It was Bashir," Mustafa said, his eyes darting between the office door and me. He was right to be scared. If his mum had any inkling he was here, she'd send him back to Gambia (which doesn't seem like a punishment, especially the way Mustafa talks about it). "It was all him. He schemed the whole thing."

Aadam nodded like a maniac. "Rumour has it that he told Miss in private that he was on the verge of a diarrhoea explosion and if he didn't go at that moment, he would live to regret it."

I had to hand it to Bashir. That was well-played.

"I heard that too," Mustafa squeaked, ducking a little when Mrs Hedley roamed towards the door. The inspectors were inside, looking very serious. "I mean, I literally heard. I was there and this was said – for sure."

"I knew it," I hissed, almost getting up from my chair in revenge-mode.

Mustafa must've noticed because his hands were already on my shoulders, firmly pinning me down. Had he not restrained me, who knows what I would have been capable of?

"Basically," Aadam began, checking the corridor for intruders (AKA Sairah). "When he was meant to be doing a number two, he snuck into the Biome and, well, the rest

is history. It was a set-up, and you were framed."

"Framed?!" I mumbled. "For a crime I didn't commit. The injustice of it all." I sat up straight, determined. "Boys, it's time for the 5B Revengers to assemble. Who's with me?"

"Not me," they both echoed.

"I'm not going up against MI5," Aadam said. "No way."

Mustafa looked more serious. Maybe he had changed his mind. "MI5 doesn't bother me." Yes!

"But my mum will . . . sorry, Yusuf," he finished. "I'm out. Anyway, you don't have time to get side-tracked. The baby delivery is coming soon, and you can't afford to make any more mistakes."

Mustafa was right and so was Aadam. I didn't have time to waste. If anything, at least I had best friends who'd always remind me of the mission at hand and would always be by my side.

At that moment, the door clicked open and Mrs Hedley and MI5 the inspectors were making their way towards me.

"You're on your own," Mustafa just about mustered as he slid unnoticed out-of-sight. "God help you."

"Ameen[13]," Aadam whispered as he melted away with him, leaving me to face the wrath of the grown-ups on my own.

13. Amen

# CHAPTER TEN

"If it were me," Amma said, waving a wooden spoon dangerously in my direction[14]. "Trust me, you wouldn't have gotten off so lightly."

I don't know if I've mentioned this already, but after yesterday's antics, I got sentenced to detention; it was on a Friday of all days too. The thing you may or may not know is that people like me don't survive in detention. In these specific situations, we were no different to goldfish in a shark tank and making it out alive was unthinkable.

"I know, Amma," I muttered, trying to assess the size of my toes. Giving her eye contact would probably just set her off.

"I'm surprised they didn't suspend you from school." Amma shook her head shamefully. "Honestly, what am I going to do with you?"

I may not have been sure about what being 'suspended' meant, but I sure as anything knew that I didn't want to

14. The kitchen wielded so many weapons that it was **ALWAYS** necessary to be **ALERT**.

Google it to find out. I didn't think my body could hack that sort of information, especially since nobody had made clear which part of the school I'd be suspended from. Big heights always gave me a queasy tummy and dangling from a huge building was not my idea of fun.

"What are you making?" I asked, trying to change the subject and then maybe her mood. Hopefully, she wouldn't detect my plan and would just fall for it instead.

Amma was slicing some red peppers. "I'm just trying to make a snack for your affa. She'll be up in a bit. She's just not having a good day today."

"I thought you were going to help Nanu shower." I scratched my head. The last I saw she was hovering outside the bathroom door, eyeing up a nail clipper with a magnifying glass.

"Ya Allah, your Nanu!" Amma's head snapped up. "I totally forgot! Poor ma. She's probably still waiting and she's on a time limit!"

And it was then that my LIGHT BULB moment happened. Remember what we agreed on before? An uncle ALWAYS takes care of his people.

"You know," I announced, sitting up straighter. "I'm going to help you."

Amma raised an eyebrow. "You're going to clip your Nanu's toenails for me?"

GROSS.

No, thank you. The last time I did that, Nanu stuck her foot in my face, and I almost swallowed a hanging toenail whole! I did not want to live through that again.

"I think I'll just stick to making Affa a snack."

I mean, how hard could it be?

# CHAPTER ELEVEN

Now that Amma had disappeared upstairs, and I had the kitchen to myself, I could unleash my inner MasterChef. I may only be ten years old, but thanks to our Ninja air fryer (yes, you heard right), a pesky Nanu, and a series of YouTube shorts, my culinary skills were unmatched by anyone but Affa and the elders.

Handesh boola[15], nooner bora[16], chicken samosa; you name it, and I could both lick it and cook it (in that order).

Today's challenge was to make something deeeee-liciously edible with the already sliced red pepper and leftover ingredients in the fridge. Amma was going for a, dare I say it, 'dull' hummus snack, but thankfully, I had a LOT more than that to work with.

A quick investigation in the fridge revealed some tasty treats to choose from:

- Cheese String and Babybel
- Khatol (jackfruit)

15. The Bengali-version of a date-pancake
16. Deep-fried ginger rice cakes

46

- An Asda pizza base
- Sheep brains
- Leftover chicken tikka jalfrezi
- Some garlicky spinach

With such a fine selection to choose from, I decided to settle for a simple red pepper, chicken tikka jalfrezi and garlicky spinach pizza with some lightly grated Cheese String and Babybel sprinkles. I'd have to save the brains for another day. I knew that Affa would be gutted about that.

I covered the air fryer basket with baking paper and piled the toppings over the pizza base inside it, shaping them into Affa's mesmerising face. Chicken tikka for eyes, a red pepper nose, spinach for hair and the cheese for Affa's spots. It was PERFECT! When Amma came to inspect it, it would be hard to tell the difference between a photograph of Affa and my chef's special masterpiece. All that was left to do was to turn up the heat.

After the ten-minute **DING,** it was sizzling, smoking and ready-to-be served.

My tastebuds were tingling. I knew this was Affa's treat, but a great chef never delivers without a little taste.

I cut a tiny slice of a HUMONGOUS bite, which thankfully was only half of the whole thing.

"Hmmmm." This was possibly the best of all my creations to date. It tasted both crunchy and spicy, sweet and garlicky, and perhaps there was a teeny-weeny hint of a little something called LOVE. "But something is still missing," I thought aloud.

And then it hit me! HOLY SNOTBALLS, I had forgotten THE MOST IMPORTANT THING!

I raided the cupboards, pushing away the dried fish heads, the half-empty pot of goor (not to be mistaken for goo AKA a Number 2) and the deadly ghost chillies. And there it was, in the middle of the mess: the seasoning tray.

Shaking my body and the little bottles, I sprinkled a dash of paprika, a smidge of some prickly green herbs, and a little pop of black pepper.

And ta-da! One extra special snack was coming right up!

I took a deep breath and an even deeper whiff, but in all the excitement, the worst possible thing happened.

I tried to stop it, truly I did, but my body couldn't hack it. The pepper zoomed too quickly up my nose and meddled with my nostril hairs only to release the HUGEST MOTHERLOAD of a snotty sneeze right onto Affa's homemade tasty treat.

# CHAPTER TWELVE

Amma's footsteps creaked lightly on the stairs. I froze. She must have been on the first step, which meant that I had about 43.7 seconds to fix this mess before she demoted me back to less than man-of-the-house material. With my uncle-status at stake here, this was something I couldn't risk, especially after the failure of my first mission.

Think, Yusuf. **THINK!**

But my mind was completely blank. My bogies had nested deeply into the cheese like a second home, and the snot had slipped across the tikka jalfrezi like a clean glaze. Had I not known that it was human remains, I might've even thought that it looked extra succulent.

## FOCUS, YUSUF. FOCUS RIGHT NOW!

My heart wasn't the only thing thumping. Amma's dull thuds were getting louder and louder and closer and closer. Any second now, she'd storm through the door, insisting to see the best bake this side of Newcastle had to offer. Yes, Amma could be that demanding when she put her mind to it! She was definitely Affa's mother.

Without a second thought, I whipped the pizza back into the air fryer and turned up the heat to dry off the excess nasal slippiness. If I couldn't clean it off, my next best (halal) bet was to suck the life out of it. At least that way my house of bogies would go unnoticed and Amma would forget all about yesterday's antics. In shaa Allah, Affa would be so proud of her snack that she'd buy me a Krispy Fried Chicken meal deal with a purple Fruit Shoot too[17]. Maybe my little treasures would even make my pizza just that much more tempting. With all these thoughts whirling through my head, I was either losing it or desperate. I guess only time would tell.

And just as Amma slipped through the door, the final **DING** of the timer echoed through the room.

17. Even on a bad day, (I hate to say it) that was just the kind of person Affa was: a generous fried chicken donator.

# CHAPTER THIRTEEN

"Yusuf!" Amma snapped, making me jump. Her eyes glittered dangerously.

I looked up slowly, holding my breath, praying it wouldn't be my last.

"Something smells absolutely amazing," she said, a smile spreading quickly through her face.

### PHEW!

"Erm," I pulled the handle of the air fryer slowly to reveal its delicacies. "It's nothing really. You won't like it. It's disgusting."

A quick inspection confirmed that there were no snot dribbles present, but there was no way I could feed it to Amma, right? Affa, I could get away with, but Amma? NO WAY.

I'd have to confess. I had no other choice. Snot-flavoured pizza should never be on an old person's menu.

"I have something really important to tell you." I looked her directly in the eye to show her how serious I was. Uncle-material people never ran away from fear. We ran towards it!

But Amma didn't even bat an eyelid. "You know, Yusuf? I'm actually dead proud of you. I know it's not been easy with your affa back, especially since things have changed so much, but I'm impressed that you're taking some responsibility." She drew up a chair and sniffed deeply. "I'll do a quick taste test, shall I? Give you the seal of approval?"

"NO!" I may have shouted just a little too loudly.

Amma jumped with a start, her eyebrows knitted together. "You don't want me to try it?" She said it softly, like she was dying and trying to decide whether to go towards the light or not.[18]

"No, no, no, no, no. That's not what I meant!" I pulled the pizza away from her, but her little glazed eyes followed it. How cruel would I have to be to say no to the being who made me?

I shook my head. "Okay, maybe just a little bit from the side then. You know how hangry[19] Affa can get. It's better not to take away the things she loves most."

I tore a small square from the jalfrezi side and tried not to pull away too much of the cheese, but (disappointingly)

18. And that, even on a good day, was the type of person Amma was - one that gives you puppy dog eyes until you give her exactly what she wants.
19. hungry + angry = hangry

53

it was extra stringy, just the way I usually like it.

"Thank you very much," Amma said, nibbling on it immediately. She chomped a few times before coming to a grinding halt mid-bite.

Oh no! She had figured it out.

I closed my eyes and prepared for the ultimate threat of the slipper.

But it never came.

"Yusuf!"

I dared to half-open one eye.

"This is scrumptious!"

"It is?"

Maybe the snot-pockets had air-dried after all!

Amma nodded proudly. "It's a little saltier and a little stringier than I'm used to, but that can easily be forgiven."

I beamed at Amma. Yes! It was just a matter of time until I earned my uncle-material badge.

But wait, I didn't put any extra salt in. Where did that come from?[20]

20. I found out the answer to that question when another huge snot-explosion splattered into my mouth. Who knew human-nasal slime was a little on the salty side?

# CHAPTER FOURTEEN

I didn't have time to think twice before a high-pitched scream, worthy of shattering a whole house of glass, pierced through the hallway.

Amma and I locked eyes on each other and froze. Ever since the baby began using Affa's body as a cosy den, she had become more and more like a starved T-Rex on the verge of extinction. We would have to feed it her quickly.

"YUSUF! I'M GOING TO KILL YOU!" Affa's voice came rattling down the stairs.

I hid behind Amma, using her body as a human shield.

"What have you done now?" she asked, forgetting about all the good I'd done already. "Go upstairs and apologise right now." She peeled me off her. "I said right now!"

Knowing my chances of surviving were slim against two enemies instead of one, I bolted up the stairs before either of them could catch me. I'd need the protection of the fortress of my man-cave if I wanted to survive.

I quickly locked the door and dragged my basket in front of it to secure the entrance. Affa's newfound hangry strength knew no bounds.

But it was useless. She burst through the door effortlessly, her hair like an octopus' flailing arms. I was steady and armed, with an Epaderm at the ready. I wasn't exactly scared of Affa, but at that exact moment in time, I had made sure that the bed was between us. Should she choose to attack, I could throw the Epaderm as a decoy and crawl under the bed, slipping just out of her reach. Flat Stanley[21] had nothing on me. Living with a bump meant that seeing the floor was just a distant memory to Affa.

"What the actual fudgecakes is this?" Affa launched a half-eaten mango in my direction.

Little did she know that my reflexes were fast enough to catch it. No way was a mango being treated like this in my household. Not while I'm man-of-the-house anyway.

But the second my fingers grasped the sweet-honey plumpness, I realised something was TERRIBLY wrong.

"GROSS!" I launched the gross little slimeball of a mango back at Affa without a second thought.

### BAD MOVE! BAD MOVE!

Affa was too slow to duck, and everything happened in even slower motion. Jumping on the bed to try and correct my mistake was AN EVEN BIGGER MISTAKE. With bees in my belly and a lump in my throat,

21. Google it.

I watched as the slippery ball of mush splattered right onto Affa's head.

"NANUUUUUUUU!" I shrieked, grabbing the covers for protection. "LA HAWLA WA LAA QUW-WA THA ILLAH BILLAH!"[22]

"Yes, Eesoof," Nanu said calmly from the corner of the bedroom. She was sitting on the floor with her tasbeeh in her lap.

For a second, Affa forgot that she was angry with me, and I forgot that I was ABSOLUTELY TERRIFIED of her, and we both SCREAMED at the TOP OF OUR LUNGS.

"Get off me, Yusuf!" Affa shouted as I wrapped my arms around her, quivering. "Nanu, when did you get here?"

"When you ask that question . . ." I told Affa, peeling myself off her disproportionate limbs. "Have you forgotten how she answers?"

Phew! At least Nanu attempting to scare the living daylights out of us meant that Affa was a teeeeeeny weeeeeeny bit calmer. At moments like this, I truly remembered how much I loved doing things with her.

"It all started before partition, way back in 1947 . . ."

22. Amma had told me that if I said this, I'd be protected. I'm not sure how protected I was feeling right now though.

"Nanu!" we both said, pulling her up from the floor together.

There's no way that a Nanu should ever be on the floor. Not under any circumstances. If there was nothing to sit on, then you had no choice but to become a horse and let her rock on your back. It's Nanu's Law. Look it up.

Affa went back to glaring at me. "Look what your grandson did to the mother of your great-grandchild.' She pulled the sticky strands in her hair and almost gagged.

"It's not my fault that she slept on the very pillow I'd used to hide the mango you weren't going to let me eat two weeks ago, Nanu."

Affa went pale. "I'm actually going to vomit."

But Nanu shook her head. "We don't have time for that today. My appointment at the opticians is in less than half an hour. We need to get a move on, otherwise we'll be late."

"How am I going to take you with this gunk all over me?" Affa picked at her hair again. "I need a shower."

"You're not wrong," I knew something smelled off, and it wasn't my P.E. socks.

"Who's going to take me, then?" Nanu asked, just as Affa slowly locked her eyes on me . . .

# CHAPTER FIFTEEN

[OPERATION UNCLE STATUS] was ALL SYSTEMS GO-GO-GO once again. This time, the rules for the mission were harder than ever. I know what you're thinking: I didn't think that was possible either.

Agent Khan (that's me) had a tricky situation up his sleeve and below is the intelligence Agent Stinkypants (that's Affa) had given me:

- Hold Nanu's hand (under no circumstances are you to let go of her hand)
- Use the zebra crossing (it's there for a reason)
- Hold Nanu's hand (under no circumstances are you to let go of her hand)
- Remember to get to the pedestrian lights and wait for the green man (even if other people are crossing when the red man is on, don't go because Nanu won't be fast enough, and you will die because I will kill you)
- At the lights, do **NOT** let go of Nanu's hand – she'll make a break for it

- Nanu's red passport date of birth is 03/02/34 - imprint this onto your brain and don't use her real birthday
- Don't let go of Nanu's hand (under no circumstances are you to let go of her hand)
- Remind the opticians to use the pictures for Nanu, not the letters - a samosa is a triangle, a nooner-bora is a circle and so on
- On your way back, repeat the above steps carefully (no shortcuts)

"Nanu?" I asked, tying one side of one of Affa's hijabs onto her handbag and the other to my belt (I couldn't afford to take any risks, could I?). "How is it possible for such a tiny person to cause so much mayhem?"

"Eesoof, beta," she said, putting her own hijab on. "I could say the same for you." She stuck a shred of red cabbage in her scarf and smiled, thinking it was a pin. "There, ma shaa Allah. I look perfect." Nanu smacked her lips and grabbed her walking stick.

I gave Nanu the handbag to make sure that we were chained together. Nothing could separate us now. Even if she was a whole three steps slower than me, my ingenious contraption meant that she would always follow my lead.

"Okay, Nanu." I took a deep breath, making my way towards our gate. "Say bismillah[23]. We're about to make our way to the dark realm of ~~Mordor~~ the HIGH STREET."

Just as I opened the gate, I heard a **HUGE PLOP!** Terrified I had done a Number 2 in public, I checked my pants. Thank God they were clean. It just so happened that Nanu's handbag had plummeted to its almost-death.

### BUT WAIT?!

Nanu wasn't attached to the handbag. Why wasn't she attached to the handbag?

With a lump at my throat and a flutter in my tummy,

23. Trust me, if you knew Nanu like I did, you'd definitely need God's help with this mission.

I quickly scanned the driveway for her presence. She wasn't in the rose bushes, under the car, or behind the wall. She was absolutely nowhere to be seen!

"Nanu, where are you?" I shrieked. My heart had decided to defy gravity and float directly to my head, making me queasy. "Where's my Nanu? What's happened to my Nanu?"

"Eesoof, beta," came a voice from behind me. "I'm just putting on my slippers. I'm a little slow at my old age."

"Oh."

PHEW. Now that I'd established that Nanu hadn't been abducted by aliens, I waited for her to put both shoes on and took her by the hand. After a whole 13 and a half minutes, we were finally at the top of the street on the long road towards Specsavers.

At first, I thought it would be gruelling, but it was actually worse. Every dog bark, every bird tweet and every car that beeped brought with it unimaginable tummy churns. My hands had gone beyond the sweaty stage and the repetitive thud of Nanu's walking stick felt like a time-bomb ticking.

Finally, I reached the crossing. Affa's instructions here were simple. Press the button and wait for the green man. But not everybody was so patient. An older boy on a scooter whizzed past while the red man flashed, nearly getting flattened by an oncoming motorbike. By the time I'd waved my hands in the air to get his attention, he had already disappeared.

"Did you see how dangerous that was, Nanu?" I said to her, shaking my head. "Teenagers these days, they think they're invincible."

I turned back to grab Nanu's hand again, but the unthinkable had already happened. In that split second of trying to save a teenage life, Nanu had disappeared for real, leaving no trace of evidence behind her.

# CHAPTER SIXTEEN

**HOLY SNOTBALLS.** THERE'S A NANU ON THE LOOSE!

I repeat: **CODE RED!** There's a Nanu on the loose!

Without a second thought, I activated spy-mode. A quick 360° only told me what I already knew: the road was getting busier, the air thicker, and there were more human bodies surging like tidal waves in my direction. Absolutely none of them, and I mean none of them, resembled a milk-chocolate Nanu.

Focus, Yusuf. Focus.

"She can't have gone far," I whispered to myself, while trying to zoom into the not-so-distance. I adjusted my glasses and tried again. "I just have to slowly retrace my steps."

Like lightning, I whizzed back up the road from whence I came. An asthma attack would be the least of my worries if I went back home without the most important branch of our family tree.

I peeked in all the alleyways, checked in all the wheelie bins, and finally fell flat to the ground to check under a delivery van.

"What if someone ran her over?" I thought I'd heard an injured animal whimpering, but looking into the wheel of the van made me realise that it was actually just me!

Oh why, oh why was this happening to me? Hadn't enough injustice fallen upon me already?!

Pull yourself together, Yusuf Ali Khan. An uncle doesn't simply lose it when he loses someone. No, a real uncle finds solutions. SO FIND ONE!

I took a deep breath and tried to turn off the leaky tap behind my eyeballs.

Breathe, Yusuf. Breathe.

I focused on the sky to steady myself. It was so big, so wide and so blue. There wasn't even one funky-shaped cloud in sight.

It will be okay. It will all be A-okay in shaa Allah.

But what if there was a dangerous dog on the loose and Nanu had been mauled viciously? Aadam had told me that he'd seen first-hand the damage some teacup yorkies were capable of.

I did another quick 360° and eyed a man loading a van nervously.

What if my beloved Nanu got Nanu-napped? What if they had tricked her with gwa-faan and coaxed her into a lorry, only to knock her out with her own walking stick?

I shook my head and rubbed my eyes to stop them burning.

No, let's be real: Nanu would not be the victim in that situation. She would be the perpetrator.

WHAT IF NANU'S KIDNAPPED SOMEONE AND IS CURRENTLY HOLDING THEM HOSTAGE?

Is this what worry felt like? If it was, I wanted NOTHING to do with it. How does Amma cope with all these voices inside her head?

My brain was whirring too fast. I had no choice but to FREEZE and sit with my feelings to reason with them.

After scouting out a clear quiet path with only a few stones for company, I took a seat on the curb and slowed down to listen to my thoughts.

"Remember what Affa says," one of my thoughts sang loudly. "When you lose something (or someone), say inna lillahi wa inna ilayhi rajeoon."[24]

I whispered it over and over again and picked up one of the stones. I know it sounds really weird, but it was like the stone was speaking to me, telling me all the secrets of the earth. If I wasn't mistaken, I had just graduated from super-spy to stone-whisperer in less than 3.58 seconds flat.

24. I know I always tell you that we also say this when someone dies, but that's not exactly out of the question with a full-scale nanu on the loose.

"Nanu's pace has quickened," I explained to myself, with an authority I didn't know I even had. It was like somebody had taken over my soul and was speaking for me. Where else could I even have got this knowledge from? "She must've let go of her walking stick."

LO AND BEHOLD, at exactly 103° to my right lay Nanu's lonely walking stick.

How had I missed that before?

I closed my eyes tightly, wiping them dry, and listened harder.

A little mumbling broke through the fuzz like an old, disconnected walkie-talkie spy-station.

"Back in my day," Nanu complained. Her voice was low, but within hearing distance.

"THERE'S A FELL VOICE IN THE AIR," I shrieked, scrambling to my feet in the direction of her words. "NANU!"

And there she was, on the other side of the busy road, waving her hands and yelling at a little boy who looked like he was about to burst into flames.

# CHAPTER SEVENTEEN

Between the whizzing cars, the stuttering buses, and the rush of people, getting to Nanu safely seemed borderline impossible.

"Nanu," I screamed over the busy traffic. I had to get her attention. If she saw me, at least she'd remain calm and stay exactly where she was. That would give me enough time to cross at the lights and rescue her. "NANUUUUUUUUUUU!"

Nanu's eyes snapped up and turned in the opposite direction. Maybe she needed her hearing checked too.

"Eesoof, is that you?" she yelled at the tree behind her. "What have they done to you? And when did you get so tall?"

I waved my arms in the air frantically, using her walking stick to draw extra attention. "No, Nanu. I'm over here. HERE!"

Nanu's eyes darted my way. Eye contact had been established. Alhamdullilah! Thank YOU, ya Rabb!

But something wasn't right. She frowned and pointed her finger at me, before raising her right hand like a swinging knife.

"Nanu?" I hugged her walking stick. That would protect me, right?

And just like that, without any warning, Nanu BOLTED down an alleyway.

**HOLY JAFFA CAKES!**

"WHAT ARE YOU DOING?" I screamed, running towards the crossing for dear life! But it was too far, and my legs were already failing me. God only knew how far she'd get if I wasted more time. I had no choice but to use the island in the middle of the road. If I didn't, Nanu would just become a dot in the distance.

After seeing the coast was clear, I got to the first safe zone the road had to offer. I checked carefully again for the next hurdle. A motorcycle whirred past me, a lorry rumbled by, and a cyclist slowed everyone down as she drew nearer to my island of safety.

I looked again for Nanu, but it was no use. I needed to get to the other side quickly.

Thankfully, after a face-off with a bus,[25] I made it to the path and sprinted down the alleyway Nanu had disappeared into.

"Nanu, where are you?" I yelled into the empty void. There wasn't a soul in sight, except for a whistling pigeon. It twisted its head back and forth, eyeing me dangerously.

Suddenly, a smoke-bomb was launched at me from the very direction the pigeon was in! It was a conspiracy! I didn't know exactly what that meant, but it sounded like the right word!

Stumbling back, I inspected the weapon of musty inhalation with my very own eyes.

It wasn't a smoke bomb at all! It was a piece of faan that

25. Clearly it was intimidated by my determined stance – I had strategically placed my big toe on the road to make it look like I would daringly run out at any moment.

had burst into flames. Who would do such a thing?

I looked up and found my answer.

"Well, well, well," a croaky voice said. "What do we have here?"

# CHAPTER EIGHTEEN

"Nanu, please," I begged, trying not to get too close. "It's me. It's just me, your beloved Eesoof."

With a quick sweep of her scarf, Nanu began circling me suspiciously.

"Prove it," she snarled, fiddling with the safety pins around her sari. This wasn't looking good.

WHAT?! How was I meant to . . . wait one smelly minute! Not only was it not looking good, but Nanu wasn't looking! She wasn't wearing her glasses! They must've fallen off when she'd made a run for it. That explained everything!

But how could I prove myself to her? I had to tell her something that only the closest people in her life knew, something totally top-secret, something even the government didn't know.

**AH-HA!** I'd got it!

"Your real name is Nurun Nessa Begum, not the one

on your red passport!" I closed my eyes, praying it would work. If not, I was a dead man. She'd think I was a spy and she'd chop me up. That would be the last of me.

There was a wave of silence that washed over the alleyway. Slowly, I opened my eyes, only to see Nanu peering into my nostrils, nearly giving me a heart-attack!

"Eesoof, is that really you?" She bent down to help me up from the ground[26]. "When did you get so short?"

**PHEW!** Disaster averted!

"Where did you learn to run like that?" I said, catching my breath. Nanu never failed to surprise me.

"I thought you were immigration, beta," Nanu replied, grabbing her walking stick with one hand and the pigeon in the other.

"Immi-who?"

The pigeon looked peaceful in Nanu's grasp.

"Never you mind," she said. "Let's get home, beta. I've caught a chicken to cook." She pointed at her pecking partner-in-crime.

We *definitely* needed to get her to the opticians STAT!

26. How did I get there? I must have fallen in shock.

# CHAPTER NINETEEN

"I just can't be responsible for something like that again," I told Mustafa the next day at school.

We were in our usual spot in the yard, and he'd taken his jumper off because it was so hot.

"I've even got a grey hair. Look!" I pulled it out of my pocket. It was my first ever one. I'd found it on Nanu's walking stick yesterday and I knew I had to treasure it forever after that. "If this isn't uncle material, I don't know what is."

Mustafa was inspecting my silver souvenir carefully when Aadam ran over to him and jumped on his back.

"Nooooo!" I yelled, trying to save my precious strand.

Thankfully, Mustafa dove like a hero to secure it. I took it from him for safe keeping. No way was I risking that again.

"Khalu's got three grey hairs," I told Aadam. The last time I saw his dad I was sure there were three peeking out of his beard. "I'm only two away from catching up to him now," I finished proudly. I puffed up my chest a little, so they knew that they were in the presence of a superior being: an uncle (that's me).

Mustafa scratched his nose. "I'm sure it's got to be on your actual head to count."

These youngsters didn't appreciate or understand the value of anything these days.

"I can do you one better," Aadam announced, pulling out a little furry cat-like substance from his bag. "Here you go - a fake beard. Now you can look like an uncle too." Aadam passed over the goods with a little superglue. "You know, for long-lasting stickiness." He grinned and patted his strangely puffed-out belly, which made him look like a little bit of a human cushion.

"Anyway, I was saying to Mustafa that my respect points were up yesterday after successfully taking Nanu to the opticians. Amma and Affa were dead proud of me, kind of. It came at a price I'm not sure I'm willing to pay in future, though." I trembled at yesterday's memory. "Nanu is just too much chaos in one tiny soul. I've never seen anyone try to cook a pigeon before."

Aadam's jaw almost dropped to the floor as, at that

very second, a pigeon crossed our path. "It knows we tried to eat its brother," he whispered. The little bird glared at him with a vengeance. "Don't worry, you creepy goose. I feel like chicken tonight anyway."

Mustafa set the record straight before I could even imagine what a pigeon and potato curry would look like. "Affa wouldn't let it in the house, so Nanu snuck it round the back. Yusuf set it free when she was distracted."

At that, the pigeon raised its wings and flew away. Clearly, its job here was done.

"Then I washed my hands. A LOT." I continued, inspecting the beard that was meant to be glued to my chinny-chin-chin. It looked like Santa Claus', but in black.

Aadam sat down against the wall and put his own chin to his knees. His face was both shiny and serious if that was even possible. "I don't get it. Why are you so obsessed with this 'uncle' mission, anyway? What's the point?" He looked up at me as my cheeks burned.

Oh great. I tried to secretly blow on myself to cool them down.

By the looks of it, it was Mustafa's turn to gang up on me now. "When the baby's here, I know you're going to be the best uncle anyhow."

Trying hard to hide my BIG smile, I turned away from them. I knew I could trust Mustafa. He wasn't my best friend for no reason. He always knew what to say.

"I mean, because you're Affa's only brother, that makes you the best by default, right?" he finished.

Oh right. Remind me to cross out that last bit about being best friends.

I turned to face them, putting my hood up to cover my pink ears. "You guys won't understand. I'm the man-of-the-house, even if Affa regrets giving me that badge now. I HAVE TO BE the best uncle. I don't have a choice. When the baby's here, he's going to need someone to look up to and someone to talk to."

"You know that he won't talk straight away, right? You've got time." Aadam interrupted, but Mustafa shushed him.

"I'll have to train him." I pulled out the sheet of pros and cons I had made about the baby when Affa had first announced it. At the time, I may have felt just a LITTLE insecure about the bean[27].

"Look, the new kid will be just like me. Think of him

27. That's according to Affa, anyway – she made me make the list. Sometimes I really do bring out the teacher in her. SIGH!

as a mini-me in the baking. I'll finally have someone to blame for my mistakes and we can team up against Affa together."

Mustafa raised an eyebrow, giving me an 'are you sure about this?' look. I guess now was the time to initiate damage control.

"What I mean is that the baby will need someone to teach him how to ride a bike, to swim, to share his Jaffa Cakes with. You know, all that really important stuff."

Aadam perked up again. "How are you going to teach him all of that when you don't know how to do it yourself? Especially the Jaffa Cake one. I still have bite marks from the time I tried to sneak one off you." He patted his belly at the memory.

Deep down, I knew Aadam was right. I didn't know how to ride a bike or how to swim. Affa and Amma were always too busy to teach me. They showed me how to paddle in the sink once, but that was about it, and Nanu forbade bikes in fear I'd run myself over. Maybe they were right. Maybe I wasn't cut out for uncle life after all.

"Yusuf," Mustafa said, popping my thought bubble. "You'll be a great uncle. I know you will." He smiled and rubbed his hands together. "Plus, it's Friday so you know what that means, don't you?"

Aadam pulled himself up and cracked his knuckles (or at least tried to before he regretted it). "We need to get to work. You've got a school to break out of."

# CHAPTER TWENTY

"Wait, what?"

Did I miss something entirely? I looked up above my head just to double-check.

"It's jummah day[28]," Aadam said, pulling up his sweatshirt and polo top to reveal the cause of his pufferfish look. "I had a feeling you'd forget so I brought my thobe as back-up. I'll take it off in the toilets at break. It might be a bit slimy though. I've been sweating all morning."

Suddenly, it all flooded back to me like a high-speed freight train:

Friday prayers . . .

Sneaking out . . .

## DETENTION!

"That's it," I said, almost falling to my knees. "I'm done for. I'm absolutely done for. I've failed. I'm never going to be uncle-material. How on planet Earth, the Sun, the stars, and the galaxies beyond am I going to break out of both detention AND school?"

28. Jummah day is on Fridays. It's when all the uncles go to the mosque to pray together.

"We could do it next Friday?" Mustafa suggested. "It might be easier then."

Good idea.

"Bad idea," Aadam piped in. "Didn't you say the baby is being delivered next week? By then, it will be too late."

"Is it too late to stop the delivery? Can we intercept it? Is there anyone in the Amazon you can call?" Mustafa asked me.

"I don't think it works like that. They just give it to you. You don't get to choose the day."

Everything was falling apart already.

Mustafa started pacing; clearly his brain was whirring at two million kilometres per hour. "Maybe you can negotiate the detention? Do it next week instead."

"Do you really think Miss Minchell will be open to negotiation with all the trouble you got her into with MI5?" Aadam rolled his eyes. "You're meant to be the smart one, Mustafa."

"You'll just have to make a break for it after you eat your dinner. Have your food then run, Yusuf. Run like your life depends on it! Don't look back. Don't think. Just go. Don't worry about us. We'll make it. We'll be okay without you. You got this!"

But even just the sound of that plan made my stomach plop to the floor.

Aadam wasn't having any of it. "You're acting like Miss won't send out a search party for you. Do you remember the time that Year 1 kid bolted through her legs and tried to make it through the car park gates? He ended up getting his head stuck between the railings, and Miss was still yelling at him while rubbing butter between his ears."

"It's not going to work," Sairah said, giving us all mini heart-attacks.

"You've got to stop doing that!" I squeaked, trying to catch my breath.

Sairah just shook her head. "One of you will have to disguise yourself as Yusuf and do the detention for him. It's the only way."

"That's a bad idea." I said.

There were so many things that could go wrong. Couldn't they see that?

"It's the only idea you've got right now," Saleem said, creeping up from behind her.

"I hate to say this . . ." Sairah began with a huge smile.

For the record, when Sairah says this, she means the total opposite. She LOVES to say it, whatever it is.

". . . But we're going to have to enlist the help of a higher power," she finished.

Saleem's head snapped up. "Do you mean . . ."

We didn't have time for this. "I've already told you that

I'm out of ideas."

Aadam shook his head. "I don't think she means you, Yusuf."

Mustafa started pacing even faster this time. A flurry of panic seemed to sweep through him. "I'm not sure that's a good idea, not after last time."

Then it dawned upon me. They weren't talking about asking just anyone. They were talking about making contact with the elusive Masked Trickster!

# CHAPTER TWENTY-ONE

"I'm with Mustafa on this one," Saleem said, following him in circles as they both paced our corner of the yard.

Sairah shook her head so hard that her plaits almost slapped her in the face. "Stop being such a scaredy cat, Saleem. It's BECAUSE of the Masked Trickster that Yusuf won Form Captain. There is absolutely no way he would've done it otherwise, even if it was against Bashir the Basher."

"Hey! I so could have won it on my own. Right, boys?"

Mustafa took this precise moment to stop pacing, only for Saleem to bash straight into him, while Aadam decided to inspect the old bite marks on his tummy. Great.

"I don't think the Masked Trickster is working right now," Saleem said. "There's been no sign of him since the election."[29]

Sairah raised an eyebrow. "How do you know the

29. Thank God too. I wouldn't ever admit it to anyone else, but the Masked Trickster gave me the shudders. There was something not quite right about someone so mysterious.

Masked Trickster's working hours?"

Saleem shrugged his shoulders.

"Are you sure we should unsettle the beast?" I asked.

Something didn't feel right about this plan; and we were doing so well on our own anyway.

"I don't think we have a choice." Sairah looked over to the other side of the yard where Mr Boakye, Aadam's class teacher, was wandering. "Look, for this to work, we need someone more intelligent than us, someone more skilled, and someone more experienced in the deceptive arts. Like it or not, the Masked Trickster is the best of us and, right now, he's the best chance you've got."

"I'll do it!" Saleem shrieked excitedly as he started jumping on his toes. "Er, I'll make contact."

Sairah eyed him suspiciously as she watched her brother run towards the library. "Great. If Saleem does that, all we have left to do is have a back-up plan to buy us time. Who's going to be Yusuf in disguise for the detention? It's not like I can do it."

"Why not?" Aadam asked.

"I'm a girl."

That made sense.

I eyed Mustafa. "Please, please, please, please, please! I'll let you borrow my Hulk Smash hands for two days; I swear to you."

"No way and no thanks." Mustafa raised his hand to make it final.

"But why?"

He was supposed to be my best friend.

"A: Because my mum will kill me."

Okay, so I knew that was coming.

"And B: Because I'm Black."

Good point.

"But who's going to be Yusuf then?" Aadam asked. "If we don't have a decoy, we can't buy ourselves more time and it's not going to work. Who's even going to realistically pass off as him?"

Mustafa and Sairah turned to Aadam, grinning like the Cheshire cat. They were thinking exactly what I was thinking.

"W-what?" Aadam stuttered. "What are you all looking at me for?"

I patted his tummy, just above his bite marks. "You know that you're my favourite cousin, right?"

# CHAPTER TWENTY-TWO

I was in the boys toilets, trying to breathe slowly.

In . . . and out.

In . . . and out.

In . . . and out.

On the outside, from the reflection in the mirror, I looked like an ordinary 10-year-old boy, with a black thobe hidden under my school uniform. Never did I think I would see the day that my superhero costume would be disguised under mortal-being clothes. The world didn't know it yet, but Spider-Bhai was getting ready to strike again.

My insides told a whole different story. My heart had jump-started into a life of its own. Within my very skeletal walls, my vital organs were performing for the anatomy Olympics. If they went any further up my throat, I would probably vomit.

Focus, Yusuf. Focus.

I had washed my hands, gargled, rinsed my nose, and splashed my face already. My arms were next, then my hair. In a public setting when non-Muslims were on the loose, it was REALLY important to wudhu[30] quickly. You did NOT want to be caught red-footed in the sink, but time was working against me.

Suddenly, there was a quick flush.

Wait! What?

When did people get here?

I swung around, trying desperately not to lose my balance as Liam clicked open the cubicle door.

We locked eyes on each other, like predator and prey.[31]

"Errr," Liam began, his eyes widening.

Don't ask me. Don't ask me. Don't ask me.

"Why is your foot in the sink?"

~~Yaa Rabb~~ [32] Oh maaaaaaaaaaaann. *COME ONNNN!*

"I have a . . . disease . . . er . . . I mean, I don't." Where was I going with this? "My foot just really . . . stinks."

Liam's eyes fell to the tail of my thobe. It must've slipped out when I was raising my feet.

"Why are you wearing a dress?"

"Er . . . yes. That is what I'm not wearing."

---

30. No wudhu = no prayer. There was no point in doing something as dangerous as this if I wasn't going to do it properly.
31. I wasn't sure which one I was either.
32. Tip #1 for embarrassing situations: never call upon your Lord in the boys' toilets of all places.

What?

I didn't have time to explain!

An awkward silence followed, and my left foot was still in the sink.

"I'm just gonna go now." With that, Liam slowly backed out.

I quickly wiped my foot before someone else crept up on me.

"Hang on one smelly minute," I said to myself.

"Did Liam just leave the toilets without washing his hands?" I tried not to gag. He was about to have his dinner too. SUPER GROSS! And here I was, worried about washing extra limbs.

At that very second, the Year 6 dinner bell rang through the toilets. I did a quick mental run-through of Sairah's plan. Saleem had managed to get the Masked Trickster on our side and all I had to do was make it to the car park gates alive.

It wouldn't be easy, and my insides already felt hollow. After supergluing the fake black beard to my face for extra deception, I looked into the mirror one last time.

Any minute now, Aadam would be making his way to Miss Minchell's classroom with his hood up, pretending he was me with a stomach ache.

Any minute now, the Year 5 whistle would blow and that would be my signal to break out.

# CHAPTER TWENTY-THREE

Stealth mode had been activated.

Melting into the shadows of the school walls and crawling on all fours to blend into the Year 1s had helped me find my way into the yard undetected. I could breathe fresh air again. Who knew how long that would last?

Phase One of the plan would be taking place in T minus 30 seconds. I just had to wait for the signal. I scanned the yard quickly for Mr Boakye and found him nibbling on his usual spicy sweet potato pasty. He was roaming around on security alert, hawk-eyeing the usual suspects. Thankfully, I wasn't one of them (for now).

"Oh my," Sairah shouted.

Phase One was now in action. I crouched down like a panther, keeping a lookout for her distress signal.

Sairah hobbled

dangerously towards Mr Boakye. "Oh," she squeaked, this time more high-pitched. "I just don't feel well. I think I got the chickenpox. Cluck, cluck!" She spun twice on the spot and waved her hands before fainting[33].

What the snotballs was that?

There was literally no way on planet Earth, the Sun, the stars, and the galaxies beyond that I could use that to advance to the next part of our plan. Mr Boakye simply walked over her without batting an eyelid.

I needed another opening and I needed to do it fast. Phase Two would initiate in T minus four minutes!

I scanned the playground again and saw a big group of Year 3 girls playing 'What's the Time, Mr Wolf?'. This. Was. Perfect. We should've thought of that!

I lay low, dragging myself undetected towards them. Timing was key.

"It's 3 o' clock," the smallest of them said. All of them (me included) took three wobbly steps forward.

"Hey!" one of them squeaked. "You're ruining the game, you beardo. No boys allowed." She shook her head and her friends glared at me like a pack of hungry pigeons.

I raised my head to give them the full force of my uncle-glory and shook my head. They froze. Not a peep

33. Well, I wouldn't call it 'fainting' since she'd crawled to the floor and still had one eye open.

came out of them, as they stared in horror at my face.

"Say it," I hissed to the smallest girl, keeping her eyes locked on me in a trance.

She quivered on the spot and whispered slowly, "What's the time, Mr Wolf?"

They couldn't see the smile behind my beard, and they definitely didn't see my next move coming.

"IT'S DINNER TIME!" I bellowed at the top of my lungs.

All of a sudden, the whole yard started squealing and running in every direction possible. Even Sairah scrambled to her feet to save herself from being crushed in the stampede and Mr Boakye's pasty splat flat on the floor as an earthquake of little people erupted around him.

It was carnage.

It was perfect.

It was time to bolt to the halfway point.

# CHAPTER TWENTY-FOUR

Phase Two of **OPERATION BREAKOUT** was led by Mustafa. It mapped out my path from our usual spot in the playground all the way up to the far-side gate, where the real escape would happen.

To the unsuspecting eye, this was a straight-forward mission, but the thing with Mustafa was that he wasn't your most reliable right-hand man. Mustafa had, what we spies liked to call, 'THE FEAR OF MUM'. Because of this, he had to be a double-agent. His role was not only to be a part of the plan, but he had to make sure he didn't LOOK like he was a part of the plan (just in case our tricks were exposed and all else failed). Dealing with Miss Minchell was bad enough. Dealing with Mustafa's mum was an unthinkable situation.

Being careful not to give my location away, I ducked behind the strategically positioned backpack and Teenage Mutant Ninja Turtle lunch box that Sairah had stolen from Lost Property[34]. Peeking over them

34. We had the intention of returning it, of course — spies, we were; thieves, we were not.

carefully, I waited for the next signal. My stomach was already turning and my need to pee was making itself known. But since I had already done wudhu, there was no turning back to empty the bladder now.

As if on cue, Mustafa's voice echoed through the playground. He was only a few metres away, but my supersonic hearing skills meant that I could make out every syllable clearly.

"Mr Boakye, I need to speak to you!" he shouted. "It's really important. My sister's social life depends on it."

Mr Boakye, who had obviously gotten over his lost pasty, raised an eyebrow and turned away from my direction, moving slowly towards our decoy. Right now, my legs were itching to run to Phase Three, but a good spy had to make doubly sure things were going to plan before forsaking the designated safe zone. After this point, the stakes were higher. If I wanted to turn back, now was the only time to safely do it.

Mustafa rummaged through his bag and pulled out the book he'd searched endlessly for in the teacher's section of the library. His voice was a lot quieter, and I could only just about make out what he was saying.

"My sister may or may not have been reading 'I HEARD WHAT YOU SAID'. He pointed to the book in his hands. (The other thing I should've pointed out about Mustafa is that he is a compulsive truth-teller so we have to be careful with him. We have to drip-feed him only the necessary bits of information lest he be held hostage by forces beyond our control.) "Word in the staffroom is that this is your favourite book, and my sister may or may not have had questions for me to ask you . . ."

Mr Boakye was locked in. Reading was his weakness. He was a sucker for a good book, and little did he know that this would be his downfall. With Mustafa now deep in conversation, it was enough of a signal for me to know that Phase Three was imminent.

Taking a deep breath and preparing myself for the run of my life, I adjusted my glasses and began the journey to the last leg of our escape plan.

# CHAPTER TWENTY FIVE

Phase Three of [OPERATION BREAKOUT] depended on the Masked Trickster, but the crusader himself was nowhere to be seen. Worse still, this side of the playground was colder, quieter, and cloudier. My spidey-senses were tingling. Something just didn't feel right.

I stripped my uniform off to reveal my black thobe and waited at the gates of the car park. It was agreed that this would be the easiest way to blend in with the railings, categorically not drawing attention to myself. Crouching down, I pressed myself as closely to the bars as possible and waited, watching carefully for any sign of movement. The screams on the other side of the playground had begun to settle and an eerie quiet made the air thick and heavy.

Where was the Trickster?

I scanned the grounds again, trying hard not to press my head against the iron padlock that hung on the gate. Getting to the other side was crucial. That would be my ticket to freedom.

But still, there was no sign of help. Had he forgotten? Had he changed his mind? Even worse, was this a trick to get me into bigger trouble? I wouldn't put it past the prank-master himself to do such a thing.

At my very moment of doubt, a gust of wind blew litter in my direction and settled between my legs. Upon closer inspection, it wasn't rubbish at all! It was a playing card! I had been in the presence of the Masked Trickster all along!

"I'm sorry I doubted you, oh masked one of the tricking kind. Forgive me." I squeezed the card close to my chest and noticed there was writing underneath the picture of the Joker. "Keep your friends close and your enemies closer," I whispered.

What did that mean?

"Yusuf Smelly Khan," said a voice from above me.

**NO WAY!**

I'm having a nightmare. I'm having a nightmare. A'oodhu billahi minash-shaytaanir-rajeem. A'oodhu billahi minash-shaytaanir-rajeem[35].

I looked up slowly, daring my eyes to deceive me, but there he was: Bashir the Basher.

35. I had no choice but to ask for God's protection from the Shaytaan (AKA Satan AKA the **DEVIL** himself).

# CHAPTER TWENTY-SIX

*NOOOOOOOOOOOOOOOOOOOOOOOOO OOOOOOOOOOOOOOOOOOOOOOOO!*

Please, yaa Rabb. Please! I DID NOT COME THIS CLOSE JUST TO BE THWARTED BY SHAYTAAN IN HUMAN FORM!

I glared at Bashir as he looked around uneasily.

"What are you doing here?" I grabbed his arm and pressed him against the gate, so he didn't draw even more attention to us. The presence of a bright blue sweatshirt would not go unnoticed while Mr Boakye was on the loose.

"Get off me." He pushed my hand away from his arm and glanced quickly over his shoulders. "Look, I don't wanna be here either, but . . . but . . ."

"But what?" We didn't have time for this!

Bashir pushed back his hair, making those spikes even more threatening (if that was possible).

"But I don't have a choice." He was shaking too. Wait, was he scared? "The Trickster put a message in my tray. He said that if I helped you out, then we're calling it squits. He said we'll be even, and he'll never tell anyone that I . . . that I . . . why are you wearing a fake beard?"

So, the Masked Trickster had dirt on Bashir. Well played, my bhai. Well played.

"The beard is sunnah[36], but how are YOU going to help?"

"I'll give you a leg over, but we have to wait for the signal."

Oh maaaaaan. I was hoping he'd have the keys or something. I guess a life of crime was never easy.

"What's the signal?" I asked, keeping my eyes glued to the main playground just in case I missed it.

As if on cue, a huge SHRIEK pierced through the air, sending a shiver straight down my spine.

"What the fudgecakes was that?" I searched frantically for the source of the noise.

"The signal!" Bashir jumped up and knitted his fingers together to make a step for me. "Saleem's just set Chompy loose in the Year 1 playground. Come on! We don't have time!"

"Holy snotballs, Bashir!"

"What!?"

"If Chompy is loose in the Year 1 playground, why is

36. It's something the Prophet Muhammad (peace be upon him) used to do.

he making a break for it in our direction?!"

Bashir's eyeballs nearly popped out of his head as he followed my eyeline. Chompy the Chameleon was indeed making a beeline our way like a wild T-Rex whose tail was on FIRE!

"Yusuf! Come on!" Bashir was panicking now. His ears were pink, and his eyebrows were twitching. He knitted his fingers together to make a step again. "If you don't leave now, you don't leave at all."

He was right. Everyone's attention had been successfully diverted.

It was now or never.

Gripping onto the railing for dear life, I pulled myself up with Bashir's wobbling hands. My insides were jelly, but I was almost there.

"Push!" I gasped,

just before hauling my body over to the other side.

I turned back around to fist-bump Bashir, but he had disappeared just like that. Just like a ghost.

Never mind that; I had done it. I had made history. I was the first person to ever break out of Western Primary School.

I ducked low to steady myself, just as another cry slashed through the air and shot straight into my bones.

"YUSUF ALI KHAN!"

# CHAPTER TWENTY-SEVEN

## BIG MISTAKE!

BIG MISTAKE!

I HAVE MADE A BIG MISTAKE!

What was I thinking? Who thought it was a good idea to break out of school?? Why did nobody stop me?!?!

Miss Minchell's voice echoed through the playground again, sending sonic waves of sheer dread through my soon-to-be-dead body.

"YUSUF ALI KHAN! WHERE ARE YOU?" Her voice was coming closer.

I was a fugitive! These railings were the prison bars I'd made myself and there was no way back.

THERE WAS NO WAY BACK!

"Inna lillahi wa inna lillahi rajeoon," I cried over and over, as real burning tears scorched tracks across my face.

How would I even get back over without a leg up? I was on my own. I WAS ON MY OWN.

Ducking behind the nearest car, I hugged myself.

"You can think of a plan," I told myself. "Just think of a plan."

But my brain was wired all wrong and my thoughts weren't making sense. NONE OF THIS MADE SENSE! Here I was, a 10-year-old boy who was deluded enough to believe he could break out of school to join Friday prayers at the mosque! What the JAHAN-NAM[37] was going through my head?!

I peeked through the railings for signs of help. I just had to get back. That was all. I just needed to get back and everything would be semi-okay.

"Yusuf!" Mr Boakye was calling now.

Oh no! The search party had begun. Surely someone could save me?!

"Mr Boakye, please!" That was Mustafa's voice, and he was pleading. Oh no! Mustafa had been caught too. My best friend! My own best friend! He was a dead man walking and it was all because of me. "Please, I had nothing to do with it. I swear on my little sister's life."

"You don't have a little sister." Mr Boakye's voice was coming too close now. "You don't think your mam's making plans to send you back to Gambia? I just spoke

37. This is the Arabic word for the actual place of 'Hell'. God knows I don't want to end up there!

to her yesterday and she's not going to be impressed."

**OH NO!** Not Mustafa's mum!

My palms were leaking bodily fluids and my heart was launching itself across my chest.

"Calm down," I whispered to myself. "Just calm down. Just go round the school and through the main gates. Buzz into reception, confess your crimes, and just explain that it was all a misunderstanding. Just a little misunderstanding, that's all."

"Not another word out of you two," Miss Minchell's voice cracked like a whip. "I don't care if Saleem is the Masked Trickster, whatever that is. Sairah, you need to pipe down and tell me where Yusuf is!"

**WHAT?!**

**SALEEM IS THE MASKED TRICKSTER?!**

No way! He is the actual genius behind the school's plots and schemes! NO WAY! My whole life had been a lie. A TRAGIC LIE! And now it was about to end in death. This was not the way I had planned to go!

"He's in the car park," Saleem croaked. "I'm so sorry! Don't tell my ammu! Please don't tell my ammu!"

"HE'S WHERE?!" Miss Minchell bellowed, sending all the air out of my lungs.

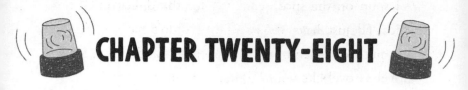

# CHAPTER TWENTY-EIGHT

ARGHHHHHHHHHH!

THEY WERE COMING FOR ME!

RED ALERT!

CODE RED!

EMERGENCY URGENT: THEY WERE COMING FOR ME!

My stomach turned inside me, and a rush of breakfast soared right up my throat. NO! Now was not the time to be sick! Gulping the bile back down, I bolted through the maze of cars and ran towards the main entrance.

If I got there before they caught me, it would be okay. I didn't know how, but that was the only thought I had to keep me going. Pushing my legs harder and faster, I rushed towards the gates.

"Yusuf Ali Khan," Miss Minchell called again. "Get here now!"

I spun on the spot, searching for the direction of her voice. I'd just have to face her. I didn't have a choice. Just put your hands up slowly and stand down, then grovel. Grovel like your life depends on it.

"Yusuf," Aadam called this time. It was his voice, even if I couldn't see him. He sounded like an angel. He would know what to do, right? My special, favourite cousin. "RUN!" he bellowed.

For some reason I would never ever understand, my body decided to follow his instructions. With my heart beating inside my throat and my thoughts overpowering my brain, I legged it across the car park . . . just as a car swung onto my path head-first.

# CHAPTER TWENTY-NINE

"You could've DIED!"

We were at home and Amma was livid. She was pacing around the sitting room all dragon-like, while Nanu sat on the sofa, tutting at me. Affa was tending to my face, trying to peel off the beard that was supposedly permanently glued to my skin.

"Explain it to me!" Amma continued, making me feel like I was little again. She raised her voice, so it hit the walls. "Tell me what in this world actually possessed you to be so foolish? How did you end up on the other side of the headteacher's car?! What was going through your head?"

In case it wasn't clear, the car that swung out at me was Mrs Hedley's. She slammed the brakes when she saw me. When I finally had the guts to open my eyes, I swear on my life that I thought she was going to run me over by choice[38]. I think the only reason why she didn't was because Chompy had found a home on my head.

Affa came to pick me up afterwards and we sat in silence on the drive home.

I kept my eyes on the floor, trying to keep my bottom lip from trembling.

"Where did I go wrong?" Amma's pacing slowed down. "I tried my best with you two and now I've discovered

38. Even though I hadn't completely ruined the inspection and our school had scraped a pass, she still hadn't forgiven me for being set-up by Bashir.

I have an ape of a son who thinks it's acceptable to scale the school gates and make a break for it. I just can't win!"

Affa stopped picking at my beard. She looked up so I didn't have to. "Amma," she said softly. Lifting my chin up, she spoke even slower. "Yusuf, what's happening? What's brought all this on?"

I wanted to explain, but I didn't have the words. They were all stuck in my throat and my jaw just wouldn't open. It didn't matter how hard I tried.

"It's okay," Affa said, pushing my hair back gently. "It's okay."

"It is?" Nanu asked, scratching her head. "I don't actually think it is."

Affa ignored Nanu (bold move). "Take your time. When you're ready, tell us what's up."

I took 13 deep breaths before I could even string a sentence together.

"DB left me in charge." I tried to keep my voice steady, but it wasn't working. "All I wanted was to be a good uncle – the best uncle."

Affa nodded slowly and Nanu raised an eyebrow. I wasn't ready to face Amma's wrath just yet, so I avoided eye contact.

"The bean, I mean the baby, needs someone to look up to, someone who's respected and someone in charge."

Affa tilted her head and tapped my fingers.

"I just wanted to be a real uncle because everyone deserves some looking out for them, right?" I braved a peek at Amma who had now sat down beside me. "Everyone should get to have a proper family beside them."

"You're nothing like your dad, footh," Amma whispered, giving me a noo-noo. "If that's what you're worried about."

Nanu's head snapped up. "Eesoof, beta, don't put all of that on yourself."

Affa nodded. "In case you haven't noticed, we are a family – and you're going to be an amazing uncle, Yusuf. You know how? By just being your wholesome little self . . . well, the self that doesn't try to cause mischief. I don't need that in my life."

I laughed, feeling like the weight of the world had stopped trying to crush me.

"I hope so."

"In shaa Allah," Amma said, reaching for the door. "I think we all deserve some chicken samosas, don't you? Come on, ma. Let's leave them be."

Nanu grabbed her walking stick and trailed after her.

I nodded. Affa was right: we were a proper family.

"And thank you for deciding that me feeling this

sad was punishment enough for my minor antics."

"Nice try," Amma called from the corridor. "No Aadam or iPad for a month. I can't believe that your daughter's son told your grandson to run, ma."

"Your sister's boy is his father's son. Fools, the both of them," Nanu agreed as they disappeared into the kitchen.

# CHAPTER THIRTY

"Do you miss Dad?" Affa asked, still picking at my beard. By the time she got it off, I'd probably have grown a real-life one on my own.

I shook my head. "I don't really remember him much."

"It's okay to miss him, Yusuf." She pulled the corner of my skin, making it burn a little .

"Is it possible to miss someone who was never there anyway?"

Affa nodded. "Can I tell you a secret?"

Honestly, I didn't know how Affa still trusted me after everything that happened, but no way was I going to miss an opportunity for juicy intelligence from her.

"I'm actually terrified of being a mam, a mum." Affa stopped fiddling with my hairy strands. "How am I going to be in charge of a tiny little life when it finally comes?"

"You're acting like you haven't done it before."

Sometimes Affa's intelligence just disappeared. One day, I have a feeling it's just not going to come back.

"And I turned out perfect," I continued. "What's there to worry about?"

At that moment, Affa yanked the beard off me.

"OUCH!"

"There you go." She smiled at my pain. There was the sister I knew and loved. "You're back to your perfect little self again."

"Thanks," I said quietly. "Thanks for giving me the privilege of naming the bean Yusuf Ali Khan the Second."

"Say what now?"

A warm gush of water lapped my fingers.

"Erm Affa," I asked, inspecting the little stream. "Why are you leaking?"

Affa's eyes snapped wider as she grabbed my shoulders. "Oh my God, Yusuf! The baby's coming!"

# EPILOGUE

Umar DB raced like he was in the Formula 1 all the way up the A1 to be efficient, and made it just in time for Affa's delivery. The baby was born just after midnight and Nanu let me stay up so we could video-call her. Affa looked like a happy zombie and Umar DB had fallen asleep with what looked like a little loaf of brown bread. Apparently, that was my nephew.

I guess I had made it to uncle-material, just in the nick of time.

THE KHAN-RAHMAN FAMILY (aka Muhammad) yusuf the second

# ACKNOWLEDGEMENTS

I actually can't believe how much has happened since Yusuf's first story was at its ideas stage. 2019 seems almost like a distant memory and I feel like a completely different person to the one who started this series all that time ago. Yusuf, his friends and his loved ones are like family to me. What I love about his mischief-making is that readers tell me that they feel the same way too. I could not be more grateful for that. So first and foremost, I want to thank all the readers who've found home in these books, all those who've found laughter here, and all those who've shared it with others (teachers, librarians, fellow authors, social media friends and all). Words cannot express my gratitude for that. I hope you know how much that means to me.

I'm not really sure what the future holds right now so I have a lot of people to thank in no particular order. Firstly, I'd like to thank Sofia Saghir for giving me an opportunity that instilled both intense imposter syndrome, and a sense of validation that I'll never forget. I'll always be a teacher at heart, but afterwards, I actually felt like an author, which is something my past-self had never even dared dream of. The Big Breakout was written shortly after that spring, so in the same breath I'd like to thank Yasmin Rahman, Sharna Jackson, Vashti Harrison and Evgenia Golubeva for their wise words and company when I felt overwhelmed. In the end, I just needed a little time and space away after all.

I'd like to thank all those who work hard to get diverse books out into the hands of readers who need them most: Scott Evans, Rumena Aktar, Ashley Booth, Vicki Fenton, Tom Slattery, Jacqui Sydney, Ayesha at MirrorMeWrite, Emma Suffield, Nicki Cleveland, Ben Harris, Laura Jackson, John Biddle, Maaria Khan, Shifa Safadi, MuslimKidsBookNook, and so many more. I wish I could name you all.

I'd also like to thank Eileen Armstrong – honestly, the conveyor belt of books you dropped off to my classroom all those years ago not only saved me a fortune, but it gave me the tools to become both a better writer and a better teacher. A thank you to Sophie Ramshaw too, for being the space to constantly bounce and borrow ideas from. Look at where Yusuf is now!

Never did I think this series would get the recognition it has either. I'd like to thank those behind the Tower Hamlets Book Awards, and those at the Lancashire

School Library Service's Fantastic Book Awards too for sharing Yusuf's story with your readers. To win and be nominated respectively has been a real honour. Thank you so much.

It takes a village to tell a story so to my agent, Polly Nolan, thank you for setting this one up and for everything you've done in between. To Eishar Brar, thank you for letting me tell the stories that I've wanted to tell all along. To Marssaié, Sophie McDonnell, the team at Knights Of, Farah Khandaker, Annabelle Wright, Catherine Ward, the team at Audible and Ali Shahalom, thank you for bringing this to life more vividly than I could have ever imagined.

To the staff and students and Lady Evelyn Independent School (Zaynab, Sana and Sheikh amongst others), I have learnt so much in such a short space of time and I know that your sincerity, support and du'a has helped me get to where I am today. Jazakumullahu khairan.

To my family, particularly my Mama and Papa Bear, I'm not even going to try and express my gratitude – you know. To my siblings, sister-in-law and Sairah Miah, thank you for always pushing me to be better. Thank you to Smeagol in particular for that – Yusuf wouldn't be the same without you. To everyone who makes the other branches of our family tree, may He always keep us close.

Finally, to the one who pestered me every day, asking me if this book was done yet; the one who came up with the plot and little moments that made it; the one who reminded me of my 'comedic genius' (albeit sarcastically); the one who laughed at the million extended deadlines, and to the one who is most likely going to criticise my use of semi-colons and commas here, thank you. Allahumma bareek. Simply put, this one is yours.

# 'MY LAUGH-OUT-LOUD LIFE' SERIES!

# BURHANA ISLAM

## Author

Born in Bangladesh, raised in Newcastle and currently residing in the outskirts of Manchester, Burhana Islam is a storyteller who is passionate about exploring themes of heritage, belonging, identity and faith in her work. She studied English Literature at Newcastle University before deciding to become a secondary school teacher, sharing her love for stories with a new generation of curious, young minds. MAYHEM MISSION was her debut children's fiction book, and went on to win the Tower Hamlets Book award 2022. She is also the author of the sequel THE DASTARDLY DUO (2022) and AMAZING MUSLIMS WHO CHANGED THE WORLD (Puffin, 2020).

# FARAH KHANDAKER

## Illustrator

Farah Khandaker is an illustrator, and designer from Bangladesh, currently based in Toronto, Canada. She enjoys exploring humor, nostalgia, and surrealism through her work with the use of bright colours and bold characters. She received her master's with distinction from Nottingham Trent University. She has illustrated children's books and editorial pieces, and published her first graphic novel CATGHOST in 2019.

**KNIGHTS OF**

KNIGHTS OF is a multi award-winning inclusive publisher focused on bringing underrepresented voices to the forefront of commercial children's publishing. With a team led by women of colour, and an unwavering focus on their intended readership for each book, Knights Of works to engage with gatekeepers across the industry, including booksellers, teachers and librarians, and supports non-traditional community spaces with events, outreach, marketing and partnerships.